Disney

5-MINUTE HALLOWEEN STORIES

Disney PRESS

Los Angeles • New York

CONTENTS

Tiana's Ghost

Halloween night in New Orleans began with a rusty-orange sunset.

"That sun looks just like a big ol' pumpkin," Tiana said, standing in the doorway of her restaurant.

"It's perfect for Halloween," her friend Charlotte said, flouncing up in a Little Bo Peep costume. "And look—those little fluffy clouds look just like your beignets!"

Tiana scowled.

"Why the frown, sugar?" Charlotte asked. "Don't you love Halloween?"

"I do!" Tiana said. "It's just . . . there's been some weird stuff going on today. You reminded me about it when you mentioned beignets."

"Weird *beignet* stuff?" Charlotte asked, laughing. "Only you would have a pastry mystery on Halloween, Tiana."

Tiana shook her head. "It's probably nothing. I made a special batch of them for my Halloween party tonight, and they've all gone missing!"

Charlotte smiled. "You know, they say the spirits walk the earth on Halloween. Maybe *they're* the ones causing this mischief!" she teased.

Tiana laughed. But she wondered if maybe Charlotte was right.

Tiana knew spirits were real. She had seen them during her adventure as a frog.

I sure hope it's not ghosts, she thought nervously.

Just then, something fluttered at the edge of her vision. But when she spun around, nothing was there!

"Did you see that?" Tiana said.

"See what?" Charlotte asked. "Tiana, honey, get your hat and let's go. We have pumpkins to carve! Apples to bob for! A party to throw!"

Tiana smiled, shrugging off her nerves. "Okay, okay," she said. "I'm ready."

First Tiana and Charlotte went to the Halloween fest at the farmers' market to carve pumpkins. But just as Tiana was putting the finishing touches on their pumpkin, she saw something strange out of the corner of her eye.

"What was *that*?" Charlotte said, dropping their pumpkin. But it was already gone.

"You saw it, too?" Tiana asked.

"I saw *something*," Charlotte said. She looked a little spooked.

Next the friends went bobbing for apples. But as Tiana came up for air, she saw it again. Charlotte shrieked. She saw it, too!

The little wisp of white was gone as quickly as it had appeared. Tiana and Charlotte stared at each other.

"I'm pretty sure you're being haunted, sweetie," Charlotte told Tiana.

As Tiana and Charlotte
walked back to the restaurant,
Tiana kept peering over her
shoulder. She couldn't shake
the feeling that there was something
following her . . . but it always disappeared
before she could get a good look!

Tiana did her best to ignore the flutters as she settled into her restaurant kitchen. She needed to work on the finishing touches for her big Halloween party.

The first step was to replace those missing beignets.

Tiana was just sprinkling powdered sugar over the fresh beignets when the lights in the kitchen flickered and went out. Crashes and shouts of surprise sounded from every direction as Tiana's staff blundered into each other in the dark.

Tiana clutched her basket of beignets tightly, her heartbeat thundering in her ears.

Swish. Something brushed her hand!

As suddenly as the lights had gone off, they came back on again.

"Tiana, what on earth?" Charlotte cried, running into the kitchen.

"Is everyone all right?" Tiana asked, looking around. Her staff all nodded shakily. There was no sign of whatever had touched her hand, but several of the beignets were missing.

Tiana had just about had enough.

"Why is this ghost haunting *me*?" she asked Charlotte. "New Orleans is full of people. What's so special about *me*?"

"Well," Charlotte said thoughtfully, "you *do* make the best beignets in all New Orleans. Maybe the ghost is just . . . hungry?"

"There's only one way to find out," Tiana said. She rolled up her sleeves and got to work on the biggest, tastiest batch of beignets she'd ever made.

As soon as the beignets were done, Tiana and Charlotte left the treats in a basket at the restaurant kitchen's back door. Then they snuck around the corner to watch.

They waited and waited. Just as they were about to give up, there was a movement in the shadows.

Tiana and Charlotte clutched each other's hands. Tiana's heart was beating so hard she could feel it in her toes. She'd never been so spooked!

The ghost moved into the light. Tiana let out a big sigh of relief . . . and then started laughing. The "ghost" was just a bunch of kids!

Tiana stepped out of her hiding place, surprising the kids.

"Sorry, Miss Tiana!" one of them said nervously.

"Trick or treat?" said another one.

"We were just really, really hungry," said a third.

"Well, then come on," Tiana said, smiling. "I've got a big Halloween party going, and you're all invited."

"Really?" the first kid asked, her eyes wide.

"Sure!" Tiana said. "After all, a trick this good deserves a treat!"

Riley's Haunted Halloween

It was fall in San Francisco, and everyone was looking forward to Halloween. Everyone, that is, except for Riley. She was finding it hard to get into the Halloween spirit. It would be her first year trick-or-treating without her friends from Minnesota.

One morning at breakfast, Riley told her parents that she would be sitting out Halloween that year. "I'm getting a little old for trick-or-treating, anyway," she said.

Inside Headquarters, Anger was fuming. "Why are we skipping Halloween? We *love* Halloween! Whose bright idea was this, anyway?"

"Take a chill pill," Disgust said. "Riley is twelve now."

"Halloween won't be any fun without our old friends, anyway," Sadness added. "They knew exactly what candy Riley likes. Without them, who will we trade with? We'll be stuck with all the bad candy, and then we'll end up with a cavity and our teeth will fall out and everyone will make fun of us and—"

Joy shook her head, interrupting Sadness before she spiraled out of control. Long Term Memory was packed full of happy Halloween memories. Surely they could have fun in San Francisco, too! "Heads up! Mom and Dad are about to talk," she said.

"Whatever you think is best, Riley," Riley's dad said. "But I bet there are some other new girls who feel the same way. Someone who needs a friend to hang out with . . ."

"Isn't there another new girl in class? Faye? I bet she'd like to go trick-or-treating, too," Riley's mom added.

"Who's Faye?" Anger asked the other Emotions, confused.

Joy turned to look at Sadness. "We can't let Faye spend Halloween alone! With no friends? And no candy?"

"That sounds terrible," Sadness said. "She'll probably sit by the window, watching all the other kids have fun without her. She'll think of her friends back home, and then she'll start crying, and then her face will get all puffy and her eyes will get red and no one will want to look at her because all the crying will make her so . . . ugly!"

"Great!" Joy said, cutting off Sadness. "It's agreed: we're doing Halloween! Now we just need to find the perfect moment to get Riley on board. Come on, guys. We can do this!"

That week at hockey practice, as Riley laced up her skates, Faye bounded over to her.

"Hey, Riley!" she said. "Um, I was thinking, and . . . do you wanna hang out on Friday? You know, for Halloween?"

"This girl is great!" Joy said, pushing a few buttons on her console. "She just walked right up and did our job for us! Plus, she clearly understands the importance of free candy."

Riley smiled. "Well, I'm not sure if I'm up for trick-or-treating, but would you want to check out the haunted house?"

Faye nodded. "Sure! That sounds like fun!"

Joy spun around. "This is going to be *great*!"

"A haunted house?" Fear said. "It won't be too scary, will it? I mean, the house won't *really* be haunted, right?"

"Of course not!" Joy replied. "There will be candy, and spooky lights, and maybe a few parents dressed up as monsters, and candy, and new friends, and candy!"

"Did you say 'monsters'?" Fear asked nervously. "Oh, no. No, no, no. I do *not* like the sound of that!"

"You had me at 'candy,'" Anger said. "Let's do this thing!"

The days flew by, and soon it was Halloween. Faye had texted Riley to coordinate their costumes, and Riley's parents had helped her pull together a very convincing pirate outfit.

Riley turned to her dad. "Arrrrr, matey! Ye'd best save some candy for me, or I'll have ye walk the plank!"

She lifted her sword threateningly.

Riley's dad raised his hands in surrender. "Shiver me timbers! What a fearsome pirate."

"Have fun tonight, Riley," her mom said as Riley ran out the door to meet Faye.

When Riley arrived at the haunted house, she looked around. Faye was waiting outside. She was dressed up as a hook-handed pirate.

"Hey, Riley! Over here!" Faye called, waving the shiny hook she wore over her hand. "Ready to go inside?"

Fear looked at the other Emotions nervously. "Suuuure. What could *possibly* go wrong in a spooky-looking house?" he said in a shaky voice. "You're sure there are no monsters, Joy?"

Joy leaned forward on the console. "In we go!" she cried happily.

Riley took a deep breath and walked up the front steps. A skeleton sat on the porch, holding a sign that read WELCOME, BOYS AND GHOULS!

Faye laughed. "So far the scariest thing about this haunted house is the puns."

Joy snorted with laughter. "I *like* this girl!"

Riley laughed, too. Then, stepping forward, she opened the door.

A woman dressed as a vampire greeted the girls. "Velcome to my lair! Please, von't you enjoy a nice treat?"

The woman held out a dark box, and the girls reached in. Inside were what felt like eyeballs!

"Ewwww!" Disgust turned away from the view screen. "Is everyone touching those? That is *not* sanitary!"

"Are—are those *real* eyeballs?" Fear stammered. "Where did they come from? Are they going to take *our* eyeballs?"

Riley was pretty sure the eyeballs were just peeled grapes and the vampire was just the lunch lady from her school. But the girls still giggled as they felt the "eyeballs" squish between their fingers.

Riley and Faye walked toward the next room.

"ROAR!" A man in a furry werewolf costume jumped out from behind the door.

"A werewolf! Joy, that's a monster! You guys lied to me! Run for your lives!" Fear screamed. But the other Emotions weren't fooled, and they held him back. It was just a man in a costume.

Riley and Faye laughed, screamed, and ran from the room.

The next room was a giant mirror maze! Faye and Riley practiced their most ferocious pirate poses as they walked through each twist and turn.

"This is cool," Faye said. "I love puzzles."

Joy nudged Sadness. "I'm getting a serious best-friend vibe here."

Riley smiled at Faye in one of the mirrors. "Hey, thanks for inviting me out tonight," Riley said. "I almost skipped Halloween this year, but I'm really glad I came."

"No way! Me too," Faye said. "But then my parents kinda hinted that I should invite you out for Halloween. They were worried you'd spend Halloween at home."

"Hold on," Anger said. "I thought *we* were helping *her*."

"I think we ended up helping each other," Sadness said sagely.

"Ugh, you're so sappy," Disgust said, teasing Sadness.

"Does it matter?" Joy said, twirling around excitedly. "We just made a new best friend!"

"Wait! My parents told *me* to invite *you* out for Halloween," Riley said. "They thought you might not be doing anything, either."

"Hmmm. I think we've been played!" Faye said. Then she smiled. "I'm having a great time! Maybe parents do know best after all . . . but don't tell my mom I said that!"

Riley grinned at her new friend.

Just then, Faye spotted something on the far wall. "Aha! Here's the way out!"

Together, Riley and Faye left the maze and made their way out of the haunted house.

"Thank goodness we made it out!" Fear cried in relief.

Faye started to say good-bye, but Riley stopped her. "As long as we're dressed up anyway, want to do a little trick-or-treating?"

"Wait, trick-or-treating? You mean we're not going home yet? We were going to go eat candy! What happened to the happy candy? Who *knows* what kind of monsters are out there?" Fear sputtered. "Ack! Is that a zombie?"

Joy turned to the other Emotions. "Still feel too old for Halloween?"

All but Fear shook their heads as Sadness said, "Nope. This feels just right."

Pinocchio

The Witch of Walddunkel Way

It was All Hallows' Eve—one of Pinocchio's favorite holidays to celebrate since he had become a real boy.

"We oughta be heading home, Pinoke," Jiminy Cricket said. "It'll be dark soon."

"But we didn't get the rolls yet," Pinocchio said.

Geppetto had asked Pinocchio to pick up a few items for dinner.

Jiminy nodded. "Let's get them," he said, eyeing the full moon rising over the forest beyond the village. "But shake a leg!"

As they walked toward the bakery, Pinocchio overheard one of his favorite villagers, Old Grauerbart, telling a story.

"Legend has it that every All Hallows' Eve, the witch of Walddunkel Way sneaks into town from her cave near Burnt Tree Cliff," Old Grauerbart said.

"What does she want?" Pinocchio asked.

"A new familiar," the old man said. "That's what she calls her animal friends. She prefers ravens, rats, and black cats. Once she chooses an animal, the creature is never seen again."

Jiminy tugged on Pinocchio's sleeve. "Let's go, Pinoke. The baker will be closing his shop soon."

Pinocchio followed Jiminy. A few minutes later, rolls in hand, the pair started for home. The sun had set and the moon glowed overhead, casting long shadows across the road.

"It's a little spooky tonight, eh, Pinoke?" Jiminy said with a nervous shiver.

Pinocchio agreed. "I wonder if we'll see the witch tonight. After all, it is All Hallows' Eve!"

Soon Geppetto's cozy cottage came
into sight. But when they entered the
house, all was still and silent.

"Anybody home?" Jiminy called out.

"Geppetto?" Pinocchio called. He
stepped over to the fishbowl. "Oh, well,
at least Cleo is here."

"Yes." Jiminy looked around. "But
where's Figaro?"

Pinocchio gasped. "What if . . . the witch took him?"

"Don't be silly. The witch is just a story," Jiminy said.

"But Old Grauerbart said the witch likes black cats!" Pinocchio cried. "And Figaro is mostly black! What if she stole him away? Why, we might never see him again!"

Jiminy gulped. What if Pinocchio was right? What if the witch was real and she'd stolen their friend? They had to get Figaro back!

The pair rushed back outside. The
forest looked darker and scarier than ever.
Pinocchio was frightened. But he was
sure that Figaro had to be even more
terrified. "We have to go to the cave
near Burnt Tree Cliff," Pinocchio
said, peering at a peak rising over
the trees in the moonlight. It
looked very far away. . . .

Pinocchio led the way down a twisting trail. The shadows were deep and dark, with almost no moonlight seeping down through the leaves on the trees. Forest creatures rustled all around. At least Pinocchio *hoped* they were just forest creatures. . . .

"Aaaaah!" Jiminy yelled as something leaped out in front of them.

"Witch!" Pinocchio shouted.

But it wasn't a witch. It was only a deer.

Pinocchio breathed a sigh of relief. "I think we scared him more than he scared us!" he said.

Pinocchio and Jiminy tiptoed onward, following
the trail as it twisted ever deeper into the woods.
They were passing beneath a broad old oak when
something overhead let out a ghostly *WHOOOO!*

Terrified, Jiminy leaped into Pinocchio's pocket.
But it was just an owl. Jiminy chuckled and
climbed out of Pinocchio's pocket.

"Look," he said a short time later, pointing with
his umbrella. "There's Burnt Tree Cliff right there."

Sure enough, the cliff rose out of the forest
just ahead. A single twisted tree stood silhouetted
against the night sky.

The two searched the cliff until, finally, they spotted a dark
opening. Pinocchio crept closer.

"AAAAAAAAAH!" he screamed as something black and fluttery
burst from the cave.

Bats! Lots and lots of bats! Pinocchio and Jiminy flattened
themselves on the ground until the creatures had all passed.

"I thought that was the witch coming for us!" Jiminy said.

Pinocchio peered into the cave. "She must still be inside."

Jiminy lit a match, and the two slowly stepped into the cave.

"Oof!" Pinocchio blurted out a moment later as he bumped into a hard stone wall. They'd reached the back of the cave.

"It's not a very big cave, is it?" Jiminy said. He turned in a circle, shining his tiny light into every nook and cranny.

"Where's the witch?" Pinocchio wondered aloud. "And, more importantly, where's Figaro?"

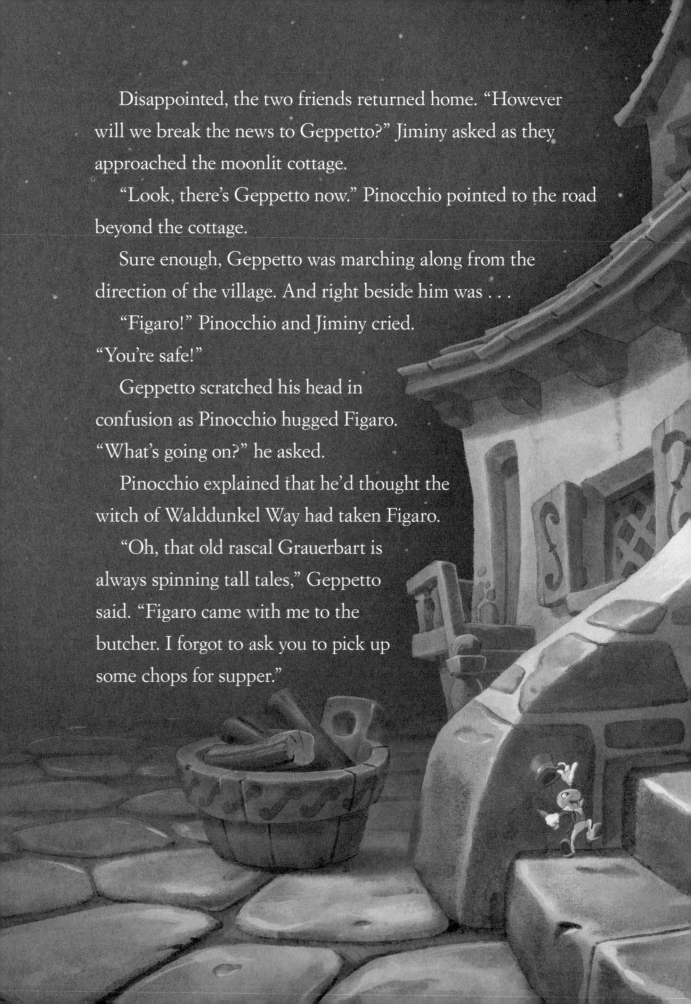

Disappointed, the two friends returned home. "However will we break the news to Geppetto?" Jiminy asked as they approached the moonlit cottage.

"Look, there's Geppetto now." Pinocchio pointed to the road beyond the cottage.

Sure enough, Geppetto was marching along from the direction of the village. And right beside him was . . .

"Figaro!" Pinocchio and Jiminy cried. "You're safe!"

Geppetto scratched his head in confusion as Pinocchio hugged Figaro. "What's going on?" he asked.

Pinocchio explained that he'd thought the witch of Walddunkel Way had taken Figaro.

"Oh, that old rascal Grauerbart is always spinning tall tales," Geppetto said. "Figaro came with me to the butcher. I forgot to ask you to pick up some chops for supper."

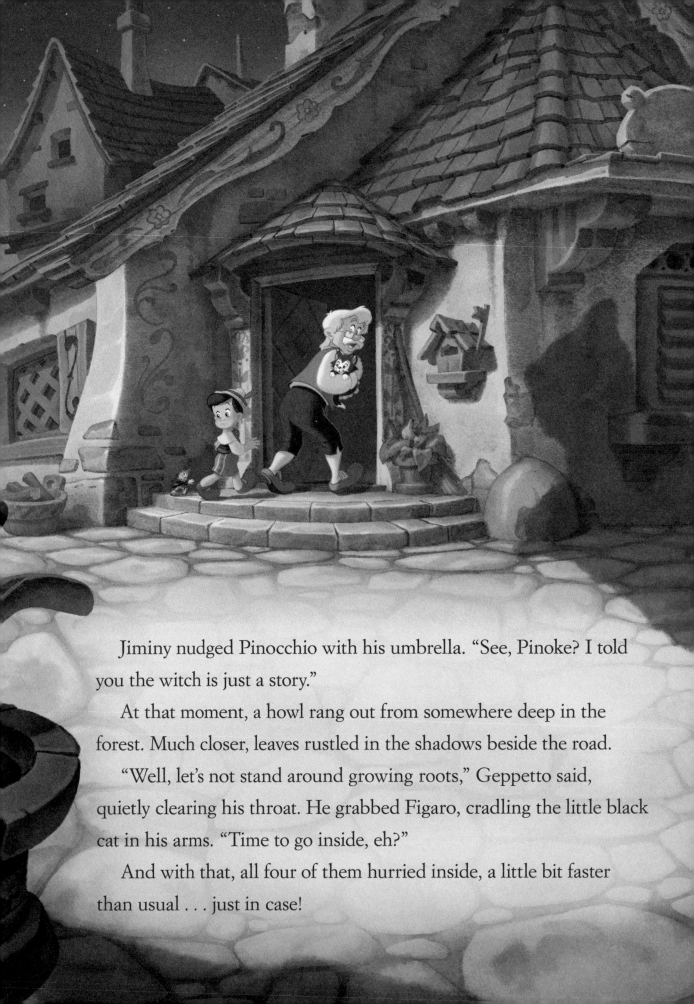

Jiminy nudged Pinocchio with his umbrella. "See, Pinoke? I told you the witch is just a story."

At that moment, a howl rang out from somewhere deep in the forest. Much closer, leaves rustled in the shadows beside the road.

"Well, let's not stand around growing roots," Geppetto said, quietly clearing his throat. He grabbed Figaro, cradling the little black cat in his arms. "Time to go inside, eh?"

And with that, all four of them hurried inside, a little bit faster than usual . . . just in case!

Boo to You, Winnie the Pooh

Once each year, there comes a most peculiar day. The dark grows darker. The leaves rattle on the trees. And everything is a tad spookier.

On this particular day, Winnie the Pooh was dressed like a bee, snacking on his last drop of honey.

"Oh, Halloween," he chuckled. "Though I'm not fond of tricking, I do enjoy treating."

A few minutes later, a skeleton bounced in.

"Not late, am I?" asked Tigger, for that was who the bouncer was. Behind him were two Eeyores—the real one, who was wrapped in bandages like a mummy, and Gopher, who had dressed up like Eeyore.

"Hello, Eeyore and Gopher," said Pooh.

"Dagnabbit!" said Gopher. "You know it's *me*?" He left to find a new costume.

"C'mon, Pooh!" cried Tigger. "We'd better get a move on!"

"But first we need to get Piglet," Pooh replied.

Piglet was putting the finishing touches on his costume when he heard a Tigger-like "Boo-hoo-hoo!" coming from his entryway.

"Why, Piglet," said Pooh as his friend hurried to greet them, "where's your costume?"

"We've got to get Halloweenin'!" said Tigger.

"Oh . . . uh . . ." Piglet stammered. He didn't really want to go outside.

"While Piglet gets ready," said Pooh, "I'll try out my costume on our friends at the honey tree."

"But, Pooh—" Piglet said, following his friend.

"Perhaps it would be best," Pooh said as he started out the door, "if you didn't say my name. It might make the bees suspicious."

But the bees knew exactly what Pooh was trying to do! They began to buzz angrily.

Pooh and the others ran away from the honey tree as fast as they could.

Nearby, Rabbit inspected his pumpkin patch.

"Perfect!" he proclaimed.

Bzzzzzzzzzzz! Suddenly, Rabbit heard the bees. He looked up just in time to see Pooh, Piglet, Tigger, and Eeyore smash into his beautiful pumpkins. The bees flew away, disturbed by all the chaos.

"Of all my favorite holidays," Rabbit sighed, "Halloween isn't one!"

Soon it grew dark, and Piglet hurried home. As he got into his costume, he realized he was just too scared to go outside.

Suddenly, there was a knock at the door.

"Who . . . who's there?" he squeaked.

"It's me . . . them . . . us!" said a Pooh-sounding voice.

"Pooh Bear?" asked Piglet. "How can I be certain it's you? Perhaps if you say something only you would say, then I'd be certain. How about 'I am Pooh'?"

"You are?" said a confused Pooh. "Then who am I?"

"It *is* you!" squealed Piglet, jumping out of his costume and opening the door.

"Piglet," said Pooh, "will you be joining us for Halloween?"

"I'm afraid I'm just too afraid," Piglet replied.

"That's okay," said Pooh Bear. "We won't have a Halloween. We'll have a Hallo*wasn't*."

"Thank you, Pooh Bear," Piglet said, smiling.

Piglet and Pooh explained their plan to Eeyore and Tigger, and with that, everyone went home.

Alone once more, Piglet created lots of notes telling all the
spookables and monstery beasts to stay away. They had to know that
it was a Hallo*wasn't* at his house somehow!

Soon a storm began to rage outside. Pooh looked out his window. "I hope Piglet isn't too frightened," he said. "I suspect that something should be done. But what?"

He tried to concentrate. "Think, think, think!" he muttered. And to no one's greater surprise than his own, he did just that!

"Just because Piglet can't have Halloween with us," said Pooh, "there's no reason why we can't have Hallo*wasn't* with him!"

A little while later, Tigger was bouncing around when two figures opened his door.

"*Spookables!*" hollered Tigger, tripping over his tail.

The spookables removed their sheets. It was Pooh and Eeyore.

"We're on our way to Piglet's to have a Hallo*wasn't*," said Pooh. "Would you care to come? We made new costumes, since the other ones were torn in the pumpkin patch."

"What are we standin' around here for?" Tigger said, snatching a sheet.

They'd almost reached Piglet's house when a tree branch snagged Pooh's bedsheet. Pooh was certain he'd been clutched by the claw of a spookable!

"Help!" shouted Pooh.

"Pooh Bear?" Piglet said, hearing Pooh's cries from inside his house.

Tigger and Eeyore, still wrapped in their ghostly bedsheets, tried to free Pooh from the branch.

"Oh, no!" Piglet cried when he saw them. "Spookables got Pooh! I must help him, Halloween or no Halloween!"

Suddenly, Piglet noticed the costume he'd made.

"I'll save you, Pooh!" he cried, putting it on.

He stumbled outside and yelled, "Boo!" as loud as he could.

Pooh, Eeyore, and Tigger looked up in horror and ran away, leaving Pooh's costume on the branch.

They ran past a startled Gopher, who was now wearing a Rabbit costume.

"Look out! Spookables!" they screamed.

Gopher looked up just as Piglet ran into him. They both went rolling after the others.

Rabbit, who had been trying to keep his remaining pumpkins dry with an umbrella, glanced up. "Not again!" he cried just before Pooh, Tigger, Eeyore, Piglet, and Gopher collided with him.

Costumes and pumpkin pieces flew everywhere.

Finally, they untangled themselves and discovered that there was not a single spookable around.

"You saved us," Pooh told Piglet. "You're here and the spookables aren't. You must have chased them away."

"Way to go, Piglet!" exclaimed Tigger.

Piglet's friends shook his hand. "Wait half a second, Piglet," said Tigger. "You aren't dressed up as anything for Halloween!"

Piglet realized he'd lost his costume in all the excitement. Then he smiled. "Oh, but I am," he said. "I've decided to be Pooh's best and bravest friend!"

"And that," said Pooh, smiling down at Piglet, "is precisely who you are."

Trick or Treat

"**E**verybody smile and say, 'Spooky!'"

Hiro and his friends posed as Aunt Cass took a picture. They were all celebrating Halloween together at the café.

Aunt Cass smiled. "You all look great!" she said. "Thanks again for helping with all the trick-or-treaters tonight."

Fred shrugged. "No problem Aunt Cass!" he said. Then he turned to Hiro. "What about Baymax? Why isn't he dressed up tonight?"

"Baymax doesn't know much about Halloween," Hiro said. "But he is all white. Maybe he could be a ghost?"

Baymax quickly looked up what a ghost was. "I am a robot," he said. "I cannot be a ghost."

Just then, the bell on the café door jingled. Two children stepped inside, dressed up for Halloween.

Baymax looked at one of the trick-or-treaters. She was completely covered in bandages.

"Your bandages indicate that you are injured," Baymax said. "I am here to help. On a scale of one to ten, how would you rate your pain?"

The little girl giggled. "I'm not hurt," she said. "This is my costume. I'm a mummy!"

Baymax scanned the girl with his sensors. "I will scan you for injuries now. Scan complete. No injuries detected," he reported.

The girl giggled again. "Trick or treat!" she exclaimed.

Baymax paused and tipped his head to the side. "What is a 'trick or treat'?" he asked at last.

Hiro slapped his hand on his forehead. "I guess I should have told you more about Halloween, Baymax. Halloween is a holiday when kids walk door-to-door wearing costumes and say, 'Trick or treat!' It's our job to give them a treat."

Hiro picked up a big bucket of candy and gave some to the trick-or-treaters.

"Thank you!" they said as they left the café.

Baymax looked at the bucket of candy. "Eating candy can lead to tooth decay, high blood pressure, and other health problems," he said. "It is not good for the health and well-being of a patient."

"Well, yeah," Hiro said. "But it's Halloween. Eating candy is a tradition!"

Baymax moved toward the kitchen. "I will find a better treat," he said.

The bell on the door of the café jingled again, and another group of costumed kids came in.

"Trick or treat!" they yelled.

Just then Baymax reappeared. "I will give you a treat," he said.

Baymax placed a stalk of broccoli into each trick-or-treater's bag. "Broccoli is high in fiber and contains seventeen important vitamins and minerals."

"Yuck!" one of the kids said. He looked at Hiro. "Is this a trick, mister?" he asked.

Hiro quickly put candy into their bags. "Don't mind him," he said. "Baymax can't help himself. He's a healthcare robot. Here's some candy. Happy Halloween!"

Satisfied, the kids ran off.

"Candy is not a healthy treat," Baymax told Hiro.

"Oh, Baymax," Hiro said. "A little candy is okay once in a while."

"It is important to maintain a balanced diet and active lifestyle," Baymax said.

"Halloween is supposed to be fun, Baymax," Honey Lemon chimed in. "It wouldn't be the same without candy."

That gave Hiro an idea. "Come on, Baymax," he said. "Let's go trick-or-treating. Then you can see what we mean."

Soon Hiro and Baymax were walking down the street. "When you trick-or-treat, you walk from house to house," Hiro explained. "Walking is healthy, right?"

"Correct," Baymax replied. "However, more pedestrian accidents happen at night than during the day."

Hiro turned on the flashlight on his phone. "We'll be safe, Baymax, I promise," he said.

The two climbed up the steps of a house decorated for Halloween. Hiro rang the bell. "Here we go," he told Baymax.

Soon a woman answered the door.

"Trick or treat!" Hiro said.

"Yes. Trick or treat," Baymax added.

The woman looked at Baymax. "Well, isn't that a fancy ghost costume you've got there!" she said. Then she put candy in their treat bags. "Here you go!"

"Wasn't that fun, Baymax?" Hiro asked as they walked back down the stairs.

Baymax scanned Hiro. "Your neurotransmitter levels are elevated. That indicates that you are happy. All that matters to me is the well-being of my patient."

Hiro sighed. "Whatever you say, Baymax. I guess you'll never understand how cool Halloween is."

"Would it make you happy if I understood?" Baymax asked. "Your well-being is important to me."

"Don't worry about it, Baymax," Hiro said.

Just then, a boy with a red nose walked past them.

Baymax stopped the boy. "Your red nose indicates that you have a cold or may be suffering from allergies," Baymax said. "Allow me to scan you for injuries."

"He's not sick, Baymax. That's just part of his costume," Hiro explained.

Baymax scanned the boy. "You are correct. There is no indication of a cold or an allergy. He is healthy."

"Yeah, I feel great!" the boy said. "It's Halloween!"

This gave Hiro another idea. "Baymax," he said. "Is he just healthy, or is he happy, too?"

Baymax scanned the boy again. "His endorphin levels and neurotransmitters indicate that he is experiencing happiness," he reported.

"Well, happiness is important, right?" Hiro asked.

"Correct," Baymax replied. "Happiness can strengthen your immune system."

"So now do you see that Halloween's not so bad?" Hiro asked.

"I understand," Baymax said. "Halloween elevates people's emotional state. That is healthy."

Hiro hugged Baymax. "I knew you'd figure it out," he said. "And that makes *me* happy."

Back at the café, Hiro and Baymax greeted more trick-or-treaters.

"I'll let you handle this one, buddy," Hiro said.

Baymax greeted each one with a wave. "Hello. Hello. Hello."

He gave each trick-or-treater one piece of candy. Then, before they had a chance to leave, he added some broccoli to their baskets, too.

Hiro groaned. "Baymax, I thought we agreed to not give out broccoli on Halloween."

Baymax replied, "This treat is good for digestion, and that one elevates the emotional state of these patients."

Hiro shook his head. It seemed there were some battles he just couldn't win.

Tangled

Marmalade Moon Night

Rapunzel sighed. Mother Gothel was away, leaving Rapunzel alone in the tower. Luckily, her best friend, Pascal, was there to keep her company.

"What do you want to do now, Pascal?" Rapunzel asked. She'd spent the day brushing her hair (which took most of the afternoon), painting a new mural on the wall, and rereading her three books. Now it was growing dark.

She glanced over at a dozing Pascal and laughed. "No, I don't think it's bedtime yet. I'm not very tired." Rapunzel strolled to the window and gasped.

"Look at the moon, Pascal!" Rapunzel exclaimed. "It looks like a giant bowl of marmalade!"

Just then, a flock of birds flew across the night sky, making a strange face in the glowing moon.

"Ohh, that is *scary*. . . ." Rapunzel shivered with glee. Suddenly, she had an idea. "I know! Let's make tonight Marmalade Moon Night! We can start our very own spooky holiday. Now we just need some creepy traditions."

First Rapunzel wanted to make a lantern that looked like the scary moon face.

There was just one problem. There wasn't anything around the tower that was very lantern-like.

"How about . . . this?" Rapunzel asked, holding up a watermelon.

Pascal watched as Rapunzel carefully started carving.

"Ta-da!" Rapunzel said when she was finished.

Pascal looked at her carved watermelon skeptically.

"All right, all right," Rapunzel said. "It's not exactly spooky. But it's not bad for my first try."

Rapunzel put it down on the table and stepped back to admire it. As soon as she let go, the watermelon rolled off the table, hit the floor, and smashed into pieces.

"Humph," she said. "Remind me next time that moon-o'-melons tend to roll."

"Now let's play a game," Rapunzel said. She glanced at the rest of the items in the fruit bowl. "These look just like the Marmalade Moon!" she said, picking up a few peaches.

She filled a large tub with water and added the peaches, which floated to the surface.

"Okay, Pascal," she said. "Try to pick one up. But no hands—or feet! You can only use your mouth."

Pascal seemed to think it over. Then his long tongue flicked out, lassoed a peach, and plucked it out of the water.

Rapunzel laughed. "No fair!" she cried. Then she took a turn. She plunged her head into the water, mouth wide open.

She came up coughing and sputtering—without a peach.

Rapunzel tried again, and again. But each time, the peaches bobbed away and out of her reach. Finally, she climbed into the tub, standing knee-deep in the water, and tried one more time. Once again, she just could not get her teeth on a peach.

Overcome with frustration, Rapunzel plopped down in the water. It sloshed over the sides and spilled onto the floor.

Now the peaches lay on the floor in a shallow puddle. Rapunzel leaned down, bit into one, and picked it up. "Aha!" she cried victoriously, taking the peach out of her mouth. "It's much easier this way!"

While Pascal munched on his peach, Rapunzel snuck away to put
her next spooky idea into action.

"Perfect!" she said, peering into the linen cupboard.

A few minutes later, Rapunzel crept out of hiding by candlelight.

"Boo! I am the Marmalade Moon ghost!" she said, whipping a bedsheet around her.

Pascal took one look at the figure that suddenly appeared, and panicked!

"Boo!" Rapunzel repeated. But her friend was nowhere to be seen. "Pascal?" she called out. Realizing she might have really scared him, she added, "I'm sorry. This was supposed to be fun—not *scary*."

Where was he?

Pascal peeked around cautiously from his hiding spot. He saw it was really Rapunzel under a sheet, and he breathed a sigh of relief.

He started to move from his hiding spot at the same time Rapunzel spotted him right in front of her.

"Aaah!" she cried, and fell over backward, startled.

"Okay," Rapunzel admitted with a laugh, "that *was* a little more scary than fun." She sat down next to Pascal on the chair. "No more tricks," she said. "I promise."

She glanced outside and saw that another flock of birds had made a whole new shape in front of the moon. Looking at it, she had an idea for some Marmalade Moon dress-up fun *without* the spookiness. . . .

Rapunzel gathered the things she needed—black and purple fabric, scissors, and a needle and thread—and got to work. "No peeking!" she said to Pascal. "I'm making something for you, too!"

Pascal seemed perfectly content to have a little quiet time. He had nearly dozed off when Rapunzel's voice woke him with a start. "Well? How do I look?"

She looked just like a witch—wearing a witch's hat she'd made herself and holding an old broom. "Witches love flying across the Marmalade Moon, especially with their little black cats!" she explained.

"Here's *your* costume!" she exclaimed, gently tying a pair of cat ears onto Pascal's head.

Pascal did not seem amused, but Rapunzel loved the way both costumes had turned out. "Perfect!" she cried, clapping her hands joyfully in front of the mirror.

Pascal cheered up when Rapunzel told him what the next part of their celebration was: eating some sweet treats. He even seemed to warm up to his costume.

So that night, high in a tower, deep in the woods, a friendly witch and her chameleon-kitty enjoyed their very first spooky holiday—together.

Peter Pan

A Trick for Hook

The weather in Never Land was the same as it always was: warm and breezy. Perfect for Wendy Darling to practice her flying. She was hovering unsteadily several feet above the ground when she remembered what day it was.

"Oh!" Wendy cried. She lost her concentration and fell to the ground with an *oof*.

"Why, it's All Hallows' Eve," she said, standing up and dusting herself off.

"What's that?" Peter asked.

"It's a holiday with all kinds of spooky things," Wendy explained. "And some not-so-spooky things, too. Like bobbing for apples."

"And turnips!" John added. "Tell him about the turnips, Wendy!"

"Oh, yes," Wendy said. "You hollow out a turnip and give it a face—"

"And put a candle inside!" Michael finished.

"That sounds *boring*," Peter declared rudely.

Wendy thought it over. "Well, *I* don't think it's boring," she said. "You know, they say that All Hallows' Eve is the night that all the ghosts come out!"

Peter's eyes widened. Now that was interesting to him. "I *love* ghosts!" he cried. "Are they *scary* ghosts?"

Wendy nodded gravely. "On All Hallows' Eve," she said in a whisper, "the bats stay home. The owls hide in their trees. Even the spiders are afraid to show their faces. That's how scary the ghosts are."

Peter shivered. "That's spooky," he said. He examined his arms. "Look, I've got goose bumps."

The children all piled into Peter's hideout as Wendy continued describing All Hallows' Eve.

"People play tricks on each other on All Hallows' Eve," she said, "and tell spooky stories."

"Like what?" asked Peter.

"Well, there was a story Papa used to tell us about a haunted turnip," Wendy said. "It gave me nightmares!"

Peter looked thoughtful. In fact, he looked like he was hatching a brilliant scheme.

"Tricks," he said, pacing back and forth. "Spooky stories. Nightmares."

Then he flew straight up to the ceiling, so fast he almost hit his head.

"I've got it!" Peter said. "We'll play an All Hallows' Eve trick on Captain Hook!"

Peter dug around under the Lost Boys' hammocks. Finally, he found what he was looking for: an old white sheet and a tattered pirate hat.

"If there's one thing Captain Hook is afraid of," Peter said, "it's the crocodile who ate his hand. But if there's one thing *all* pirates fear, it's the ghost of the Old Sea Dog."

"Who's that?" Wendy asked nervously.

"He's from a scary story pirates tell each other," Peter said, "a legend. He was supposed to have been the wickedest and cruelest of them all."

Peter tossed the sheet over his head and tossed the pirate hat over that.

"We're going to make Captain Hook think that the ghost of the Old Sea Dog is haunting Never Land this All Hallows' Eve," he said.

"Woooooooooooooo," Peter added in a high, spooky tone. "Shiver me timbers!"

Wendy shuddered. She knew Peter was under there, but it was still a bit scary!

Peter, Tinker Bell, Wendy, and the boys snuck down to the beach as quietly as they could. Evening had fallen, and they stuck to the shadows as they went. When they reached the water, Tinker Bell sprinkled Wendy and the boys with pixie dust. The group rose into the air, gliding silently above the waves. Soon they had reached the *Jolly Roger*.

"Shhhh," Peter whispered as they flew quietly around to the wheel, where Hook stood, looking out over the deck of the ship.

The night air was still, and the sound of the ocean lapping at the sides of the ship was faint. Wendy, Peter, and the boys hovered silently in the shadow of the ship, breathing as quietly as they could manage.

Aboard the *Jolly Roger*, Hook shifted from one foot to the other. The shuffle of his bootheel on the deck was eerily loud.

"All Hallows' Eve," Hook muttered to himself. "I *hate* All Hallows' Eve."

"What's that, Cap'n?" came a jaunty—and unexpected—response from the shadows.

Hook jumped a mile in the air.

"Smee!" he yelled. "Don't sneak up on me like that!"

"Sorry, Cap'n," Smee said. "I forgot how you hate All Hallows' Eve."

"It's bad enough having that crocodile skulking around," Hook whined. "Now I have to watch out for ghosts on top of it?"

Hidden from sight, Peter winked at Wendy.

"*Woooooooo,*" Peter moaned softly, still hidden at the side of the ship.

"What's that?" Captain Hook called sharply.

"*Wooooooooooooooo,*" Peter added, a little louder.

"Who's there?" cried Smee.

"It is I," Peter said. He rose quickly to the deck, his sheet fluttering in the ocean wind. "The Ooooooold Sea Dooooooog!"

He flew straight at Hook, moaning and screeching.

"*Odsbodikins!*" Hook screamed, and flung himself to the deck.

Laughing, the children fled as fast as they could. The look on Hook's face had been priceless.

"Where's Peter?" Wendy asked when she and her brothers landed on the beach.

The boys looked around, but Peter was nowhere to be found.

"Let's get home," Wendy suggested. "Maybe he'll meet us there."

But as they approached Peter's hideout, the hair on the back of Wendy's neck began to stand up. They could see an eerie glow through the trees. A glow like . . .

"Boo!"

Wendy gasped as a ghastly face appeared in front of them. A
grinning head with no body, it bobbed and staggered through the air.
It was . . . *a floating turnip?*

"I tricked you!" crowed someone with a familiar voice.

Peter stepped out of the shadows, laughing so hard he was clutching his sides. Next to him hung the turnip, attached to a string.

Wendy sighed. "Peter, you really frightened me!" she scolded him. "But it *was* a good trick," she added.

"That was the idea!" he said. "After all, it's All Hallows' Eve! Why settle for *one* scare when you can get *two*?"

Mickey's Slumber Party

"Pluto, I have a wonderful idea!" Mickey Mouse said one rainy afternoon. "Let's invite our friends over for a slumber party tonight!"

Pluto barked happily. They had been stuck inside all day, and he was ready for some excitement.

While Mickey called his friends, Pluto dragged sleeping bags and pillows into the living room. Soon he and Mickey were ready for the party.

Daisy, Minnie, and Donald arrived just as the rain began to come down harder.

"I brought hot cocoa!" Minnie said, pulling out a thermos. "And mini-marshmallows!"

"Just the thing for a rainy day like this," Mickey said, guiding his friends to the warm fireplace. He poured a mug for each of them.

Daisy looked around. "Where's Goofy?" she asked.

Mickey frowned. "He couldn't make it," he said.

Outside, the wind was blowing hard enough to make the trees sway. Storm clouds covered the moon. Bolts of lightning zapped through the darkness, illuminating the raindrops splashing down.

"You know what it's the perfect weather for?" Mickey asked. "Scary stories! And I know just the one to tell."

As the friends got comfortable, Mickey turned off the lights and began his story.

"Not long ago, in a village not far from here, there lived a young man who wanted to be a magician. The villagers laughed and told him that magic wasn't real. But he worked hard, and finally he was able to make things disappear!

"The villagers still did not believe in his magic. When he made things vanish in front of them, they accused him of tricking them. The magician was angry that no one believed him, and so he began to make the villagers disappear, one by one.

"Soon everyone in the village had disappeared. But the magician had grown to enjoy making people vanish. So now he wanders the land, looking for more victims. He points his long arms at anyone he sees and—"

BOOM! A huge crash of thunder shook Mickey's house, and the front door flew open. A great gust of wind blew out the fire, and everyone screamed.

"It's okay!" Mickey reassured them as he got up to close the door. "It's just the wind!" He tried to flick on a light, but nothing happened. "The storm must have knocked out the power. I'll go find some flashlights."

Minnie giggled. "I was so caught up in Mickey's story, I thought it was the magician coming through the door!"

Soon Mickey came back with a candle. "This is the only thing I could find," he said. "I don't know where all the flashlights could be."

"Mickey, where's Pluto?" Daisy asked as the candle lit up their circle. The four friends looked around, but Pluto was gone.

"Pluto?" they called. There was no answer.

The friends got up and began to look around. Donald even opened the front door and shouted into the rain. "Pluto!"

"Maybe it really was the evil magician who caused the lights to go out!" Daisy whispered. "And he made Pluto vanish!"

"Don't be silly, Daisy," said Minnie, looking around nervously. "That was just a story Mickey made up to scare us. Right, Mickey?"

Just then, the door to the basement creaked open. Mickey, Donald, Daisy, and Minnie jumped and turned in time to see a floating white shape entering the room.

"It's a ghost!" Donald cried.

"He's going to get us!" Daisy gasped, hugging Minnie.

The white sheet slipped away to reveal a familiar face.

"It's only Pluto!" Mickey said happily, going to help his friend. Pluto had gone to the basement to find flashlights. His mouth was full of them.

Daisy hugged Pluto as he and Mickey passed out the flashlights. "I'm so glad you're safe!" she said. "We've been scaring ourselves with silly things while you were gone. We thought the evil magician made you disappear!"

"I think I've had enough scary stories for one night!" Mickey said.
"What should we do now?"

"I know," Minnie said. "Since we have all these flashlights, why
don't we make shadow puppets?"

"That sounds like fun!" Donald said. "How do you make them?"

"I'll show you," Minnie replied.

Minnie helped Donald move his hands into a particular shape. Then Mickey held up the flashlight behind them, and a shadow turtle appeared on the wall!

"Wow!" Donald exclaimed. He moved his fingers, and the turtle's head bobbed up and down.

"Daisy, hold your hands like this," Minnie said. When Pluto raised his flashlight behind them, a rabbit appeared next to the turtle. Daisy wiggled her fingers, and the rabbit's ears moved.

"Now we can act out the story of the tortoise and the hare!" Minnie said with a smile.

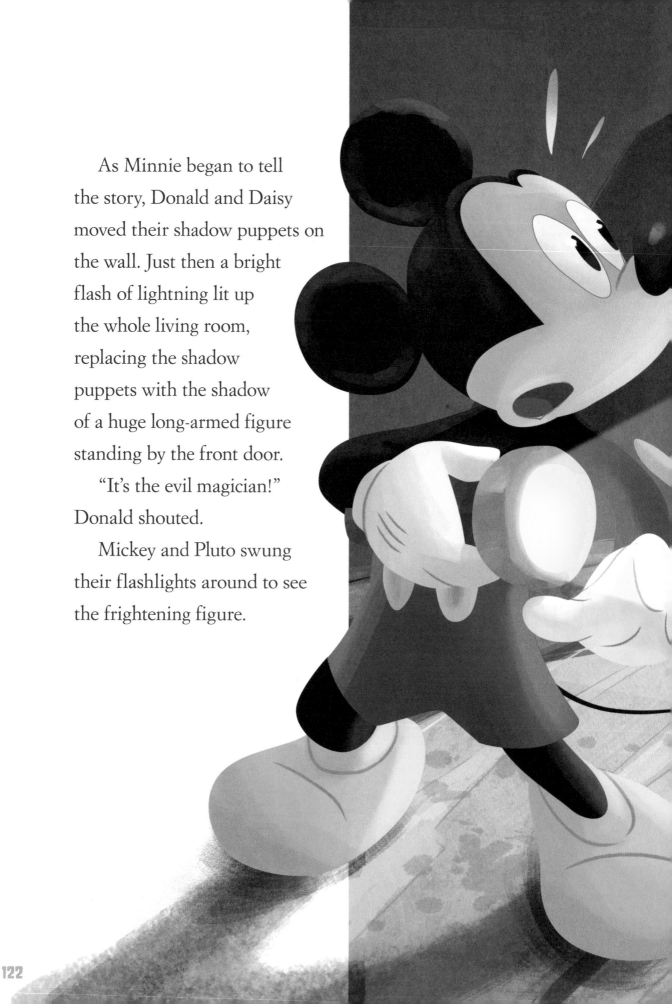

As Minnie began to tell the story, Donald and Daisy moved their shadow puppets on the wall. Just then a bright flash of lightning lit up the whole living room, replacing the shadow puppets with the shadow of a huge long-armed figure standing by the front door.

"It's the evil magician!" Donald shouted.

Mickey and Pluto swung their flashlights around to see the frightening figure.

"Gawrsh," Goofy said as he stepped through the door, taking off his wet poncho. "I didn't mean to scare ya. But it turns out I can join you for the slumber party after all! Say, who turned off the lights?"

"Mickey told us a story about an evil magician who makes people disappear," Minnie said. "We thought you were him."

"That sounds scary," Goofy said. "I know another scary story if you want to hear it."

"No!" the friends all shouted together.

Goofy held up his guitar. "How about a few songs instead?"
he asked.

Minnie nodded. "I think a sing-along is much safer than
telling stories," she said. Mickey lit the fire again, and as the
wind and thunder calmed outside, the friends sang together.

Soon everyone was yawning. The friends snuggled up in their
sleeping bags.

"Good night, everyone," Mickey said.

And with the sound of soft rain filling the room, they all fell asleep.

Cinderella

A Costume for Cinderella

It was a crisp fall afternoon. Cinderella was reading in her room when there was a knock on her door. It was Prudence, the castle's head housekeeper.

"Excuse me, Your Highness," Prudence said, "but this delivery just arrived for you. The messenger asked me to apologize. It seems this was meant to arrive much sooner."

Prudence handed Cinderella an elaborate gold box, then excused herself to see to the castle staff.

Cinderella opened the box. The inside was lined with soft velvet. At the bottom, sitting atop a small pillow, was a scroll tied with a red satin ribbon.

Cinderella set down the box and took out the scroll. It was an invitation from the king and queen of a nearby kingdom to a masquerade ball.

"How exciting!" Cinderella cried. Her mind filled with costume ideas.

Cinderella looked more closely at the invitation and gasped. "Oh, no," she said. "The ball is tomorrow night! What am I going to wear?"

"Don't worry, Cinderelly," Gus said.

"We can help!" said Jaq.

"Thank you," she said. "I'll need all the help I can get. We'd better hurry!"

Cinderella and the mice went upstairs to her royal wardrobe. Cinderella's closet was stuffed with gorgeous ball gowns, rows and rows of shoes, and more hats, gloves, and jewelry than she could count. But she didn't have any costumes to wear.

"There must be something in here we can turn into a costume," Cinderella said. "But where do we begin?"

Jaq and Gus were already hard at work, thinking of things to pair together. "We'll find you something, Cinderelly," Jaq said. "Don't worry!"

"How about this, Cinderelly?" Gus said, pointing to a few different items in her closet. "You can be a pretty flower."

Cinderella put on the hat and gown Gus had picked. Then Jaq ran around her, tying some green ribbon around her legs. Soon Cinderella looked like a flower.

"Hmmm . . ." Cinderella said, looking at herself in the mirror. "It's a nice try, but I don't think this is quite right. Plus, I'm not so sure I can walk in it!"

"What about putting these together, Cinderelly?" Jaq asked.
He pointed to a frilly white gown, a fluffy white coat, and a feathery
white hat.

Cinderella put on the outfit. "What am I?" she asked, looking at
her reflection in the mirror.

"You're a cloud!" Jaq exclaimed.

"Oh, I suppose I am," Cinderella said. "I'm not sure this is quite
right, either."

"I think we're going to have to make a costume," Cinderella said. "And I know just the thing!"

Cinderella and the mice got to work. They cut out colorful swatches of fabric and sewed everything together. Finally, all the pieces of Cinderella's costume were ready.

"It's perfect!" Cinderella said, twirling happily as she looked at her reflection in the mirror.

"Cinderelly is a very beautiful butterfly," said Gus and Jaq.

There was just one problem left. Prince Charming was away. Cinderella didn't have a date for the ball.

"Thank you for helping me make a costume," Cinderella said. "I think I know just how to repay you. Would you like to come to the ball with me?"

Jaq and Gus clapped. "Cinderelly take us to the ball!" they cheered.

Cinderella was excited for her friends to join her. "I know just what you should wear," she said.

The next evening, Cinderella, Gus, and Jaq got ready for the ball. Cinderella wore her butterfly costume. Gus and Jaq were tiny caterpillars.

"You make quite the trio!" Prudence said, showing them to the door. "I hope you have a wonderful time!"

When Cinderella and the mice arrived at the masquerade ball, Cinderella looked around. All the guests wore incredible costumes! Cinderella's costume wasn't the fanciest or the most beautiful, but she didn't mind one bit. She liked her homemade costume best of all.

Most important, Cinderella had the very best company.

"Let's dance, Cinderelly!" Gus exclaimed.

Cinderella smiled as they stepped on to the dancefloor. Soon she, Gus, and Jaq were dancing the night away!

On the carriage ride home, Cinderella and the mice were very tired. But they were also very happy.

"Thank you for being there for me," Cinderella told Gus and Jaq. "And thank you for being such charming dates!"

"Anything for Cinderelly," Jaq said.

Gus agreed. "That's what friends are for!"

Disney·PIXAR MONSTERS, INC.

Scariest Day Ever

James P. "Sulley" Sullivan and his best friend, Mike Wazowski, were on scare duty at Monsters, Inc. Sulley stepped through a door and looked around. There was no one there.

"Uh, Mike," Sulley said, poking his head back through the door. "This room's empty."

"What are you talking about?" Mike said, shoving past Sulley into the room. "This kid's always asleep by now."

Sulley shrugged. "I guess we should go back to Monstropolis. I've got lots of other kids to scare tonight."

But as Sulley turned toward the door, his tail knocked it shut.

Meanwhile, on the Scare Floor, George Sanderson and his right-hand man, Charlie, were working the same neighborhood as Mike and Sulley. They saw an activated door, but no one appeared to be manning it.

"Huh," Charlie said when he saw the unmanned door. "Looks like Mike and Sulley accidentally left this one on."

"We'd better turn it off," George said. "It isn't safe to leave a door to the human world active."

Back in the human world, Sulley reopened the closet door. But when he did, all he saw was the inside of the closet.

"The door back to the Scare Floor isn't working," said Sulley. "We're going to have to find another house with a working door . . . and fast!"

Mike and Sulley crept through the house and stepped outside.

"Remember," Sulley said, "don't touch anything!"

Mike nodded. All the monsters knew humans were toxic. But as he looked around, he realized he didn't see any humans. Instead, the streets were full of monsters!

"What's going on?" Mike asked, scratching his head. "Are we back in Monstropolis?"

Suddenly, Mike and Sulley heard a voice behind them. They spun around. A small monster was standing there, peering up at them.

"I like your costumes!" she said before running off.

Mike and Sulley looked at each other. Costumes? What could possibly be going on?

Mike and Sulley looked back at the street. There weren't *only* monsters walking around. They also saw a ghost, a black cat, a pumpkin with legs, and all kinds of other creatures.

Suddenly, one of the monsters pulled off its face. Mike and Sulley gasped. It wasn't a monster after all! It was a child wearing a mask! They weren't back in Monstropolis. They were surrounded by human children wearing disguises!

Sulley did his best to stay calm. "We have to find a door back to Monsters, Inc., now!" he said.

"George is working this neighborhood tonight, too," Mike said. "If we can catch one of his doors in time, we can get back through!"

Mike and Sulley tried to find a way inside one of the nearby houses, but it wasn't easy! They had to dodge children left and right, and there were people at the front doors of almost all the homes.

Mike and Sulley managed to sneak into a few houses, but none of the doors inside were powered up.

In one house, they got to the bedroom just as George was leaving.

"George!" Mike and Sulley shouted, racing for the open closet door. "Wait for us!"

But they weren't fast enough. George hadn't heard them.

Click! The door closed behind him.

Mike and Sulley opened the closet door, but there was no Scare Floor behind it—just a closet filled with children's clothing.

Mike and Sulley were beginning to worry. They needed to get back to Monstropolis before one of those kids touched them!

"It *is* getting late," Mike said. "Do you think any of the doors back to the Scare Floor are still in use?"

"I sure hope so," Sulley said.

Then Mike and Sulley noticed a house with no one around. The front door was flung wide open. Maybe this was their ticket home.

"Come on, let's go!" said Sulley.

Mike and Sulley tiptoed inside the house. But as they crept toward a door, they heard sounds of talking and laughter. The house wasn't empty like they'd thought.

"Oh, no," Sully said when he realized what was going on.

"We're in the middle of a party!" Mike exclaimed.

"Whoa," said someone behind Mike and Sulley. The two spun around. A boy stood there, staring at them. "Cool Halloween costumes!"

Mike and Sulley slowly began to back away. "Uhhh, Mike?" said Sulley. "It's Halloween?"

"Oops," said Mike. "I guess I missed that memo."

"Hey!" the boy called to his friends. "Come check out these cool monster costumes!"

Mike and Sulley shrank backward as a group of children approached them. "Your costumes look so real!" a little girl exclaimed. "Can I touch the fur?" She reached a hand toward Sulley.

Mike shrieked.

"No!" Sulley roared.

Sulley had forgotten how big and frightening he was. The kids screamed at the tops of their lungs and ran away.

But Mike and Sulley were the most terrified of all!

"Let's get out of here!" Mike shouted.

He and Sulley turned and ran.

Mike pulled Sulley into the closest bedroom and slammed the door behind them. "Please, please, please let this door work!" Mike said.

"What are the chances George is using this door?" asked Sulley.

"Slim," said Mike. "But we have to try."

Mike and Sulley crossed their fingers. Then they opened the closet door, and . . . it worked! They walked back onto the Scare Floor at Monsters, Inc.

Mike and Sulley breathed huge sighs of relief. They'd made it home safe!

On the other side, they found George and Charlie.

"What are you guys doing coming through this door?" asked George. "I was just about to scare the kid on the other side."

"You saved us," said Sulley. "Our door was broken."

"Oops," Charlie said. "We thought you left it on by accident and we shut it down. Sorry!"

"It's okay," Mike said. "We're back now. But whatever you do, do not go through that door."

"Why not?" George asked.

"It's Halloween, and there are kids everywhere!" Sulley explained.

Mike shivered. "Halloween is the scariest day *ever*!"

Happy Holler-ween!

The crisp fall air made Alice shiver as she walked through the apple orchard. All around her, people were picking apples for the All Hallows' Eve festival that night.

Alice quite enjoyed the festival. People bobbed for apples. They told spooky stories about spirits. And they carved faces into turnips to scare the spirits away.

Alice was thinking about scary spirits when she heard someone yell.
"WHEEE HOOO!"

The sound was coming from inside the trunk of a hollow apple tree.

"Hello?" Alice called into a hole in the tree. "Is somebody in there?"

"HOW DEE HOOOOOO!" the voice hollered.

Curious, Alice stepped inside the tree. Soon she found herself falling down, down, down.

Alice landed in a dark passageway. Pushing open a door, she found herself back in Wonderland. In front of her were the Mad Hatter and the March Hare. They were sitting at their tea table and yelling at each other.

"HOO DEE HOO HOO!" cried the Mad Hatter.

"WEE HAAAAAA!" shouted the March Hare.

"My goodness, you're both yelling quite loudly!" Alice exclaimed. "Whatever is the matter?"

"Why, there's nothing the matter," answered the Mad Hatter. "In fact, everything is quite wonderful. It's Holler-ween!"

"Don't you mean All Hallows' Eve?" Alice asked.

"I do not," the Mad Hatter replied. "Tonight is Holler-ween! It's the night when everyone hollers at each other. Like this."

He turned to the March Hare and hollered loudly. "HOO DEE HOO!"

"HOW DEE HOO HOW!" the March Hare hollered back. Then he looked at Alice. "It's your turn!" he said.

"Oh, heavens, no," Alice replied. "My governess says that children must never holler!"

"But it's Holler-ween!" the Mad Hatter said. "Hollering is a tradition. You must!"

"I suppose, if it's a tradition," Alice said. She cleared her throat.

"Hoo dee how?" she said, unsure of herself.

"If you're going to holler, you've got to be louder than that!" the Mad Hatter said.

Alice took a deep breath. "HOO!" she cried.

"Not bad!" the Mad Hatter said. "But it needs a little more pizzazz!"

Alice sighed. "I'm afraid I'm just not any good at hollering. Are there any other Holler-ween traditions?"

"Sure!" the Mad Hatter replied. "We bob for ice cream!"

"Ice cream?" Alice asked. "But you're *supposed* to bob for apples!"

"Well, that's silly," the Mad Hatter said. "Who wants to catch an *apple*?"

The March Hare nodded and scooped a ball of ice cream into a large bowl of water on the table. Then he stuck his face in it! When he came up for air, his whiskers were wet and there was ice cream on the tip of his nose.

"Doesn't that look like fun?" the Mad Hatter asked Alice.

"It looks quite messy," she replied. "Are there any other traditions?"

"Why, yes," the Mad Hatter answered. "We carve teacakes!"

"Teacakes?" Alice asked. "But you're supposed to carve turnips!"

The March Hare looked confused. "No, no. I'm sure it's teacakes," he said.

The Mad Hatter picked up a teacake and used a spoon to carve a silly face in it.

"What are you supposed to do with that?" Alice asked.

"Why, you eat it, of course!" said the March Hare. He took the teacake from the Mad Hatter and popped it into his mouth.

The Mad Hatter clapped his hands. "And now it's time to tell toast stories!" he announced.

"*Toast* stories?" Alice asked.

The March Hare nodded and lifted the lid of a teapot. The Dormouse popped out. In a small squeaky voice, he began to recite:

"Hey doodle doodle,
I like to eat noodles
And porridge and pudding and ham.
But if I have none,
There's nothing as fun
As a fine piece of toast with some jam."

When the Dormouse finished, the Mad Hatter and the March Hare cheered.

Alice clapped politely. "That was a very good poem, but it was not a proper story at all," she said. "In fact, you're not doing *anything* properly. This is not how to celebrate All Hallows' Eve."

The Mad Hatter shook his head. "We told you, it's Holler-ween!"

"Well, I have never heard of Holler-ween," Alice said. "Where I am from, it is All Hallows' Eve. And we do not tell toast stories. We tell stories about ghosts."

"Gh-gh-ghosts?" stammered the Mad Hatter. "You mean like spirits? Specters? Phantoms?"

"Yes," Alice replied.

"Ghosts, with spooky glowing eyes, that appear out of thin air?" the March Hare asked.

"Exactly," Alice replied.

"You mean like that ghost, over there?" the Mad Hatter asked, pointing.

Alice turned around to see two yellow eyes floating in the air.
Beneath them was a round open mouth.

"Boo!"

"Good heavens!" Alice cried. Frightened, she jumped backward.
The Dormouse jumped back into the teapot. The Mad Hatter and the
March Hare ducked under the tea table.

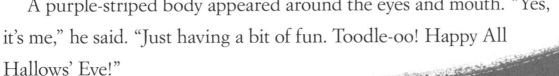

Alice's heart pounded quickly as the yellow eyes floated closer to her. Suddenly, she realized something.

"Those eyes look very familiar," she said. "Is that you, Cheshire Cat?"

A purple-striped body appeared around the eyes and mouth. "Yes, it's me," he said. "Just having a bit of fun. Toodle-oo! Happy All Hallows' Eve!"

The Cheshire Cat disappeared, and the Mad Hatter and the March Hare climbed out from under the table.

"If that's what happens on All Hallows' Eve, I'll stick with Holler-ween, thank you!" the Mad Hatter said.

Alice was still trembling from the Cheshire Cat's trick.

"I believe I agree with you," she said. "Happy Holler-ween!"

"HOO DEE HOO!" hollered the March Hare.

Tricky Treats

"**H**appy Halloween, Vanellope!"

Vanellope von Schweetz looked up and grinned. "Ralph!" She jumped into her friend's large arms for a hug.

"Hey!" Ralph said. "Did you miss me?"

"Nah," Vanellope replied. She tweaked his nose, then leaped down to the ground. "Why would I miss a big, clumsy fleabag like you?"

"I dunno," Ralph replied. "Probably the same reason I missed a snarky little know-it-all like you." He ruffled her hair.

Vanellope *had* missed Ralph. Her friend spent most of his time in *Fix-It Felix, Jr.*—the video game where he lived. She was so happy he'd come to *Sugar Rush* for Gloyd's annual Halloween party.

"C'mon," Vanellope said. She grabbed Ralph's hand, dragging him toward her candy go-kart. "Let's go for a ride!"

"What about the party?" Ralph asked.

"We can be fashionably late," Vanellope replied, hopping into the driver's seat. Ralph climbed onto the back of the kart.

"Ready?" Vanellope asked. She gunned the engine.

Ralph grinned. "Ready!"

Whoosh! They were off.

"Whooo!" Vanellope whooped as they tore around a turn. The kart skidded on two wheels for a moment.

"Gah!" Ralph yelled. He clutched the fender to keep from falling off. Vanellope grinned. Then Ralph yelled again, and this time he sounded *really* surprised.

"Pumpkin!" Ralph cried.

"Pumpkin?" Vanellope said. "What are you talking about?"

Then she looked around her. "Where are we?"

The go-kart track was gone. Ralph and Vanellope had been taken somewhere else. Somewhere *spooky*.

"I have no idea," Ralph said. "It happened when my head hit that floating pumpkin."

"Jumping jelly beans!" Vanellope yelled. She couldn't believe it!
"This must be the Halloween bonus level where Boo Bratley lives! I
thought it was just a myth!"

"Boo who?" Ralph asked.

But before Vanellope could make a joke about Ralph crying . . .

"WoooOOOooo!"

Vanellope and Ralph jumped a mile. A marshmallow ghost had
appeared out of nowhere!

"Boo Bratley!" Vanellope exclaimed, pointing to the ghost. "The meanest, brattiest ghost in all of *Sugar Rush*. Legend has it he was exiled to this bonus level many Halloweens ago."

"Soooooo haaaaaappy you've heeeeard of me," Boo Bratley taunted. "Tooooo bad that won't help you goooooo hooooome."

"Hey, wait a minute!" Ralph leaped off the kart. "We need to go back."

"You neeeed to caaaaaaaatch meeeeeeee first," the ghost moaned. Then he floated straight through the graham cracker castle doors and out of sight.

"Come on!" Vanellope yelled as Ralph opened the castle doors and climbed back onto the kart.

Vanellope and Ralph zoomed into the castle. They raced past dancing licorice brooms sweeping up cotton candy cobwebs and little jack-o'-lanterns grinning at them from the windowsills. Boo Bratley flew farther and farther ahead of them.

"Bet you can't caaaaaaaatch meeeeee," Boo Bratley shouted.

"We'll see about that!" Vanellope muttered under her breath.

She stomped on the gas, and they sped through the castle at lightning speed. The chase led them up marzipan ramps to the attic, down wobbly gummy-worm ladders to the dungeons, out to a candy-corn maze, and back into the castle again.

"Bet you can't caaaaaaaatch meeeeee," Boo Bratley repeated at every turn.

"*Argh!* If he says that one more time . . ." Ralph groaned.

"It's my caaaaatchphraaaaaase," the ghost called over his shoulder.

Finally, Boo Bratley floated right through a castle wall with no doors or windows.

"Hold on, Ralph!" Vanellope yelled. She gunned the engine so they could drive up and over the chocolate stone wall.

But midway up the wall, the kart started to fall. It wasn't supposed to carry that much weight!

"Ahhhhhhhhh!" Vanellope and Ralph fell crashing to the ground.

"Tee-hee-heeeeeee!" They could hear Boo Bratley laughing from the other side. "Looks like you're not goooooinnng hooooommmme!"

"Argh!" Ralph said, rubbing his backside. "We're *never* going to get out of here. And I've got butterscotch hay in my pants from that stupid candy-corn maze."

"I have an idea," Vanellope said. She whispered it in Ralph's ear so Boo Bratley couldn't hear.

Ralph grinned. He raised his fists and started smashing at the chocolate walls. Stones cracked and bittersweet shards flew everywhere. Soon Boo Bratley wasn't laughing anymore!

Vanellope waited for just the right moment as Ralph distracted the ghost with his wrecking. Then she closed her eyes and concentrated. *Zap!* She glitched over to the other side of the wall, where Boo was sneaking away.

"Ha!" Vanellope said. She tapped him on the shoulder. "Got you!"

"WINNER!"

Fireworks went off, and sirens blared. Vanellope and Ralph had beaten the Halloween bonus level!

A candy-cane doorway suddenly appeared. "Ready to go back to *Sugar Rush*?" Vanellope asked. Ralph nodded. But before they could walk through the doorway . . .

"Wait!"

Boo Bratley floated up to Vanellope and Ralph. "Please don't go," he said. "Won't you stay for a little while?"